INTERESTING FACTS ABOUT DOGS

1) Dogs dream in pictures and review the events of the day in their sleep.

2) With their great sense of smell, dogs can pick up on our feelings and detect changes in the human body.

3) Even if a dog sees a predator in the distance, it will not feel fear until the predator is close.

4) To calm down an anxious dog, it's better to stroke it than pat it.

5) When there is a threat, a dog barks louder and faster than how it barks during play.

6) Dogs learn their owners' habits and have a sense of time.

7) Dogs have sweat glands between their paw pads, which explains why their feet smell like corn chips.

8) A dog's u      about the
   size, sh   arby.

9) Dogs can understand about 250 words and gestures.

Waylon!

Even More Awesome

~~~~~~~~~~~~~~~~~~~

Gift of the
Hackbarth Foundation

~~~~~~~~~~~~~~~~~~~

Waylon!
Even More Awesome

SARA PENNYPACKER

PICTURES BY
Marla Frazee

𝕯𝒊𝒔𝒏𝒆𝒚 • HYPERION
Los Angeles   New York

A special thank-you to Daniel Shintaku for hand-writing our endpapers

Text copyright © 2017 by Sara Pennypacker
Illustrations copyright © 2017 by Marla Frazee
All rights reserved. Published by Disney • Hyperion, an imprint of Disney Book
Group. No part of this book may be reproduced or transmitted in any form or
by any means, electronic or mechanical, including photocopying, recording, or
by any information storage and retrieval system, without written permission
from the publisher. For information, address Disney • Hyperion, 125 West End
Avenue, New York, New York 10023.
First Edition, October 2017
1 3 5 7 9 10 8 6 4 2
FAC-020093-17258
Printed in the United States of America

This book is set in 13-point Garth Graphic Regular
Designed by Michelle Gengaro-Kokmen
Illustrations created in Black Verithin pencil on Dura-lar polyester film

Library of Congress Cataloging-in-Publication Data

Names: Pennypacker, Sara, 1951– author. Frazee, Marla, illustrator.
Title: Waylon! : even more awesome / Sara Pennypacker ;
    pictures by Marla Frazee.
Description: First edition. Los Angeles : Hyperion, 2017.
Summary: Waylon and Baxter share in the care of a stray dog,
    Dumpster Eddy—Provided by publisher.
Identifiers: LCCN 2016013924 ISBN 9781484701539
Subjects: CYAC: Friendship—Fiction. Dogs—Fiction.
Classification: LCC PZ7.P3856 Wam 2017 DDC [Fic]—dc23
LC record available at https://lccn.loc.gov/2016013924

Reinforced binding
Visit www.DisneyBooks.com

*To Caleb, for plugging me
back into science.*
    ——S.P.

To grokking.
    ——M.F.

1

One look at Baxter's face, and Waylon knew. "Dumpster Eddy was picked up again."

Baxter nodded miserably. He stamped slush off his boots and stepped inside Waylon's front hall. "About an hour ago. In a Dumpster behind Pizza Palace."

"Is he okay?"

Baxter nodded again—this time with a little smile. "I was hanging out with my dad in the police station when they brought him in. He practically wagged his tail right off! It took me ten minutes to calm him down enough so I could dig the pepperoni out of his ears." Baxter sniffed the air. "What's cooking?"

"Vindaloo," Waylon answered, pulling his coat off the hook. "Let's go see Eddy."

Baxter sniffed again. "Is it good? It smells good."

Vindaloo *was* good. So good that Waylon made an exception from his No Spicy Foods! rule for it. But he didn't tell Baxter this. "Let's *go*," he said instead, shooting his arms into his coat sleeves.

Baxter leaned into the kitchen. "Hi, Mr. Z. That smells great."

Waylon's dad saluted Baxter with his spoon and went back to stirring. Just then, a timer buzzed.

Mr. Zakowski dropped the spoon and tore into his writing studio.

"What's with him?" Baxter asked.

"He's a little nuts these days. He's waiting to hear if he sold his screenplay. He cooks nonstop, except every fifteen minutes, when he checks his email. He says that if he didn't set a timer, he'd check his email every three seconds, and he'd never get anything done." Waylon pulled on his gloves. "Come *on*. I want to see my— *our*—dog before they close up."

Baxter took a last longing sniff before letting Waylon drag him to the door. They ran the whole twelve blocks to the police station, never mind the ice and slush. Well, Waylon ran, and Baxter kept up.

But just before they reached the station, Waylon drew up short. He pointed to the sign above him. "*This* Pizza Palace?" he panted.

5

"They nabbed him *here*?"

Baxter doubled over, hands on his knees. "Yep. This. Pizza. Palace," he puffed.

"But it's so—"

"Close. To the station. I know."

"And last time, they got him behind Rosie's Bakery. Which is . . ."

Baxter nodded. "Only two blocks from the station. The other direction."

Waylon looked at Baxter. He could tell Baxter

was thinking the same thing he was. They took off even faster than before, ran up the steps to the police station, and spilled into the lobby.

When the dispatcher caught sight of them, she pulled out a ring of keys. "You two look like you need to see a dog right away." She chuckled as she unlocked the big door next to her desk.

Waylon and Baxter flew in. Midway down the hall of cages, a scrappy brown dog began barking in a higher pitch than the rest. Baxter stepped away—he always seemed to know when Waylon needed alone time with Eddy— and Waylon lifted the latch on the door. Eddy flew into his arms and knocked him over.

Waylon laughed as he let Eddy lick his whole face, every square inch. Dumpster Eddy was a thorough dog. When Waylon could finally sit up, he put Eddy in his lap and shook his finger. "What were you thinking? How come you don't run far away when we bust you out of here?"

Baxter dropped down beside Waylon. He gave Eddy a head scratch, and Eddy gave him a chin slobber in return. "Maybe he doesn't know where he is."

Waylon shook his head. All the science in him (which was a lot—Waylon was as science-y as Dumpster Eddy was thorough) rejected that possibility. "Dogs have great navigation skills. Scientists think they sense the earth's magnetic fields, like a compass. No, Eddy knows just where he is."

"Well, then, maybe he *wants* to get caught. Sometimes criminals who have spent a long time in prison don't feel comfortable on the outside anymore. When they get released, they commit another crime to get back in."

Waylon thought it over. Baxter was an expert in all things criminal, so maybe he had a point.

But finally he said no. "He loves to run too much," Waylon explained. "He hates being locked up."

"Hey, why don't you try that *grokking* thing," Baxter said. "Find out why he's letting himself get caught."

If anyone else had said *Try that grokking thing*, Waylon would have worried he was being made fun of. But Baxter wasn't doing that. Baxter understood: *grokking* was a science fiction term that meant to connect with something so totally that you practically merged with it, and Baxter knew that Waylon and Eddy grokked each other.

Waylon placed his hands on Eddy's head in mind-meld position and gazed deeply into his eyes. What he found there at the center of Eddy's soul hit him hard.

"What?" Baxter asked. "What's wrong?"

"It's our fault! Yours and mine. Eddy's *letting*

himself get caught, so he can be with us."

Just then, the Animal Control officer came in through the back door, dragging a sack of kibble. "Got to kick you out, boys," she called, rubbing her back. "Visiting hours are over."

"A few more minutes, Meg?" Waylon tried.

"Not tonight. I've got a ton of paperwork to do. Sorry."

Waylon gave Eddy a final hug, and then he and Baxter left. Once outside, they drew up their hoods. Sleet needled through cones of light spilling from the streetlamps.

"So, that's why he busted out of Desmond's garage," Waylon said as they turned onto the street. "It was so far away, we couldn't visit him every day."

Baxter nodded. Desmond was the guy who washed the windows at Waylon's condo. He had taken Eddy for them in November, but Eddy had escaped after just a week. "Nothing I could do, boys," the window washer had said. "That dog's a runner." Which Baxter and Waylon already knew, of course.

Dumpster Eddy had been in and out of the stray animals' lockup since September. It was always the same pattern: for ten days, Eddy lived in the lockup. Waylon and Baxter took turns taking him out for walks before and after school and on weekends. For those ten days, Eddy's life was the best they could make it.

The problem came on the eleventh day.

After ten days, Meg sent unclaimed strays off to whichever shelter in Massachusetts had room.

Eddy wasn't the kind of dog that would get

12

adopted from a shelter. Cute little puppies got chosen. Eddy, it had to be admitted, was homely. Plus, anyone could see he had the itch to run. What happened to dogs that didn't get adopted was so terrible neither boy ever said it out loud.

So, by the eleventh day, they had no choice but to smuggle Eddy out of the lockup. Whenever they could, they hid him somewhere, but he never stayed long before bolting. When they didn't have a place to stash him, they simply had to let him run free. They were always torn between relief and terror as he streaked out of sight.

Sooner or later, a call would come in about a dog scavenging in a Dumpster, and the police would go pick him up. It wasn't hard to capture him—Eddy always sprang joyfully into the cruiser, grinning as if to say *What took you so long?*

"We need a place nearby this time," Baxter said. "He won't run if we visit him every day."

Waylon nodded. There was nothing else to say. Waylon's mom was allergic to dogs, and Baxter's apartment was No Pets. They'd asked everyone they knew, but since Desmond, no one had wanted to take in a dog for them. The boys walked on in silence until Waylon's building loomed over them.

Baxter sniffed up toward the fourth floor. "I can smell that vindaloo stuff from here," he claimed.

Waylon turned away from the hopeful look on Baxter's face. He kicked at a chunk of ice. "What are we going to do? About Eddy?"

Baxter shrugged. "Same as always, I guess. Bust him out ten days from now. Hope he can take care of himself until he's caught again."

They watched the sleet freeze onto the sidewalk. Waylon shivered. Baxter tightened his hood. The last time they'd freed Eddy, it had been a sunny December afternoon, so warm they'd peeled off their jackets. Over the last few weeks, though, winter had hit hard.

Waylon climbed the front steps to his condo. "Ten days. We have until next Thursday to figure it out."

2

Wednesday morning, Waylon got to school early and stationed himself at the Pit to wait for Baxter.

The Pit was the alcove of lockers where the fourth graders kept their stuff. Arlo Brody, king of the fourth grade, had named it the Pit on the first day of school. Since he was Arlo Brody, king of the fourth grade, the name had stuck, even though the place was nothing like a pit of any kind—peach, barbecue, or arm.

In the Pit, for the first time in their school careers, the fourth graders had fifteen minutes of No-Teachers-Around time. Fifteen minutes between when the school doors opened and the Get-In-The-Classroom bell rang.

Everything important that happened in school happened in the Pit. Friendships were born and died. Secrets were whispered, jokes were spread, and lunches were swapped and stolen.

And plans were made.

Waylon silently practiced what he'd say when Baxter got there. *I know it's your day,* he'd begin, *but can I come with you to see Eddy?* Dumpster Eddy had been gone over two weeks this last time, and Waylon had missed him more than ever. He'd barely slept last night, his Eddy-ache had been so bad.

Charlie came in and started unloading his stuff into the locker beside Waylon's. And

Waylon remembered something that Dumpster Eddy's return had totally wiped from his mind. Waylon pulled a blue notebook from his backpack and handed it over. "*Cosmo-Quest*, Volume One: 'Pluto Landing.' I finished it yesterday."

Charlie took the notebook and bowed. "Time for my comedic genius!"

Waylon and Charlie had been brainstorming their comic book all year. The story line—Astronaut

Char-Lon voyages around the solar system with his pet monkey, Asteroid—would provide plenty of hilarious astrophysical adventures.

Waylon had never told Charlie this, but he was planning on sending a copy of *Cosmo-Quest* to Neil deGrasse Tyson. Neil deGrasse Tyson was the greatest living scientist in the world. Neil deGrasse Tyson would appreciate a comic about astrophysics. Maybe he'd even make it a regular feature on his web page.

Waylon had spent the past week researching the science for the first chapter. Now it was time for Charlie to insert some jokes and do the drawings. Charlie wasn't so great at drawing comics, it was true, but he sure was funny. Neil deGrasse Tyson seemed like a guy who would like a good laugh.

Charlie slid the notebook into his own backpack as the first bell sounded. "Supposed to snow tonight. If school's canceled, I'll work on it all day," he promised as he went into the classroom.

Baxter walked in then. Waylon slammed his locker shut and hurried over.

"Any ideas?" Baxter asked. "About where we can put Eddy?"

"No," Waylon admitted. "But about him . . . Can I ask a favor?"

Baxter peeled off his gloves. "Sure."

Waylon steeled himself. But before he could speak, the second bell rang. Mrs. Fernman stuck her head into the hall and waved them in.

The favor would have to wait until lunch.

But when the noon bell rang, Mrs. Fernman sent Waylon to run some papers to the science room. There, Mrs. Resnick asked him if he had any ideas for projects to enter in the Science Fair in April. Waylon told her his top-ten possibilities, but he kept stealing glances at the clock. Lunch period was only twenty-five minutes long.

When he finally got to the cafeteria, he looked all around. He filled his tray and slid into a seat beside his friend Clementine. "Where's Baxter?" he asked her. Clementine knew everything that went on at school.

"Principal's office. Mrs. Rice pulled him out of the line. Something about guts in her briefcase. Sounds like an awesome prank. Were they human?"

Waylon popped open his milk container. "I don't know."

"Why not?" Clementine asked. "He didn't tell you?"

Waylon sized up the items on his plate. When he was younger, he used to make his food do battle before he ate it. Now, he only analyzed

which stuff would win. The mashed potatoes could take the chicken nuggets any day, he decided. They were thick enough to wall off the peas, wait out any siege. "It's not like we're friends," he answered, without looking up.

Clementine dropped her fork. "You are *so* friends with him. You did that thing with that dog in September, and since then, I've seen you leave school with him lots of times."

Waylon shook his head. "It's still about that dog. Whenever he's locked up, we take care of him—but separately. I get Tuesdays, Thursdays, and Saturdays. Baxter gets Mondays, Wednesdays, and Fridays. But he goes to the station whenever his dad's on duty, so on my days, we're walking there at the same time is all."

"Nope," Clementine said. "I've seen you. You guys do friend-walking."

"What do you mean? What's friend-walking?"

Clementine reached for Waylon's spoon. She placed it beside her own, with their bowls leaning in toward each other. "Friend-walking." Then she moved the bowls apart so the spoons made a *V*. "Not-friend-walking. See?"

Waylon didn't answer.

"So, you *walk* like friends. Are you just pretending?"

"I'm not pretending. I like Baxter, but . . ."

"What?"

"Well . . . haven't you noticed he knows an awful lot about criminal stuff? He checks *Encyclopedia of Crime* out of the library every week. He's memorized the FBI's Ten Most Wanted list. He's visited the scene of every bank robbery in Boston!"

Clementine shrugged. "So what?"

"So, he makes me feel a little . . ." Waylon peered around. He didn't mind telling something like this to Clementine, because she never made fun of him. But some of the boys might. "Nervous."

Clementine lifted a single shoulder, as if shrugging was too much effort for something so unimportant. "I make lots of my friends nervous. They're still my friends."

"Really? You don't make me nervous." Waylon

stopped to think. It was true that Clementine spent a lot of time in the principal's office. Not as much as Baxter, but a lot. Still, he'd known her since kindergarten, and he knew she never did anything really bad. "Who do you make nervous?"

"You know Mitchell's sister, Margaret?" Clementine asked, twirling a carrot stick. "When they first moved into our building, she was a wreck whenever I was around. She used to fake heart attacks when our parents made us play together. She'd get so pale, her mother would check for a pulse. She's my friend, though. Ask her."

"Margaret doesn't count," Waylon said. "She gets nervous around dust. Who else?"

Clementine turned to the girl sitting on her other side. "Maria, do I make you nervous?"

"Sure," Maria said. "You're a trouble magnet.

I'm afraid some of that trouble's going to splatter onto me."

"But you're still my friend, right?"

Maria sucked on her milk straw and nodded.

"And does my trouble splatter onto you?"

Maria sucked on her milk straw and shook her head.

Clementine turned to Waylon. "If Baxter's criminal stuff makes you nervous, don't do any criminal stuff."

Waylon went back to his lunch. Clementine might know everything that was going on at school, but she didn't have a clue about what was going on in his life.

3

Finally, after school, Waylon got a minute with Baxter in the Pit. He drew a steadying breath. "I know it's your day," he began, "but could I come with you to see Eddy? I won't—"

"Sure."

"You can hold the leash. I won't even . . . Wait. Did you say 'sure'?"

Baxter nodded. "It's good, actually. Now Eddy won't be lonely when the chief calls me into his office."

Waylon took a step back. Being called into a police chief's office sounded as ominous as being called into a principal's office. Then he relaxed. The important thing was, Baxter truly didn't seem to mind that Waylon was butting in on his Eddy day.

Still, once they were inside the lockup, Waylon held back to let Baxter open Eddy's cage.

Except Baxter didn't. He rattled the handle. He shook it hard. "It's locked. Why is it locked?" he yelled. "It's not supposed to be locked!"

A round man in an Animal Control shirt rolled out of Meg's office holding a clipboard.

Baxter ran to him. "Why is the cage locked?" he cried. "Where's Meg?"

"Maternity leave. I'm her replacement." The new guy looked over at Waylon. "What are you boys doing in here?"

Waylon stroked Eddy's neck through the cage bars. "It's okay. I'll get you out in a minute," he promised. He hurried down the hall, trying to ignore Eddy's yelps. "Meg had a baby? When's she coming back?"

"A couple of months."

Waylon pointed to Eddy, who was frantically trying to dig under the door. "We take care of that dog whenever he's here. But the cage is locked. Can you—?"

"*Whenever* he's here?" The new officer sucked in a cheek and cocked his head. "He's been here *before?*"

"Never mind," Baxter cut in. "But please don't lock his cage. We're going to take him for walks while he's here—all ten days."

"Ten days?" The new guy leaned up against a cage and rubbed his back against the bars. "What ten days is that?"

"The ten days you keep a stray before you turn him over to a shelter," Waylon said. He heard his voice rise. Eddy was whimpering now, and the sound hurt. "You know—the rule."

"Ten days? Might have been Meg's rule. But, as I think you can see, I'm not Meg." The replacement guy chuckled as if he had made a good joke. Then he looked over at Eddy for the first time. "And anyway, from what you're saying, that mutt has already had plenty of ten-day vacations here. He'll be off to . . ."—he looked down at his clipboard—"the Springfield Animal Shelter on Tuesday."

"Tuesday?" Baxter gasped.

"Springfield?" Waylon added. "But that's . . . Where *is* Springfield?"

"About a hundred miles from here. You boys need to clear out. I've got work to do; it's my

first day. Maybe you can take that dog for a walk tomorrow."

"Can't we stay?" Baxter tried. "We'll help feed the dogs—Meg lets us sometimes."

The new officer put a hand on his hip and drew himself up. "I told you, I'm not Meg," he said again. And this time he wasn't chuckling.

Outside, the boys sank to the marble steps of the station. Dusk settled around them like a cold blanket, and they hunched their shoulders against the wind.

"It's not fair," Waylon said after a while. "Why did Meg have to go and have a baby?"

"We have to put up with Officer Sure-Not-Meg for a couple of months," Baxter agreed with a shake of his head. "And now we have to get Eddy out by Tuesday."

There was another moment of silence as the bad news sank in. They'd run out of places to put Eddy weeks ago.

Which meant they were going to have to set him loose.

Waylon looked at the sky. "It's supposed to snow tonight. Maybe eight inches." He shivered, picturing Eddy's still-kind-of-patchy coat. "Of course, snow's not the problem."

"What do you mean? How would *you* like to be outside all night in the snow?"

Waylon explained the science. "A layer of snow is about ninety percent air, trapped

between the crystals, so it's good insulation.
People live inside igloos, and they stay warm."

Baxter stood up. He kicked at a ridge of ice.
"Great. One tiny problem: Eddy can't build an
igloo."

"I know." Waylon sighed and got to his feet.

He tugged his collar up and started down the steps.

Then he stopped. He turned to face Baxter. "No, Eddy can't build an igloo," he said, feeling a grin slide across his face. "But *we* can."

4

Waylon woke up to a silence so deep it could mean only two things in a city as noisy as Boston.

He patted around his ears. No, his head was *not* encased in osmium, the world's densest material, whose atoms are so closely packed together that sound vibrations don't penetrate it. And that left . . .

He jumped out of bed and ran to the window. Yes! Snow!

Snow, and lots of it. Mrs. Gluckman on the floor below was sweeping it off the kale in her window box, and a few people on the street were stabbing shovels into car-shaped mounds, but otherwise his neighborhood was thickly coated in perfect white.

Waylon had lived his whole ten years in a city that saw a fair share of winter storms, yet the whiteness amazed him every time. Snow was made up of frozen water crystals, which were translucent, so wouldn't you think it would be clear?

He knew the science of it, of course: when light photons hit snow, 80 percent of them bounced back, and they bounced back equally along the color spectrum. White was the result of a reflection of all colors. Still, the blank whiteness of fresh snowfall was always a surprise.

Waylon dressed in a hurry, doubling up on

shirts and socks. He skidded into the hall and was just reaching for the phone when it rang.

"Corner of Beacon!" he cried into the receiver.

"See you in fifteen!" Baxter fired back.

Waylon hurried into the kitchen to grab an apple and leave a note. But his dad was just opening the oven, and the aroma that came out almost knocked Waylon over. The human nasal cavity has about five million scent-receptor cells, and he could feel all of his jostling for a front-row seat.

"Cinnamon scones," his father said, bowing over the tray.

Waylon leaned in for a deep sniff. "So you haven't heard about the screenplay yet."

"Not yet. School's canceled, by the way. It's just you and me. The subway's tied up, so your mom left early, and your sister's sleeping in. Sit down. I'll frost these."

"Can't." Waylon stepped into his boots and started lacing them up. "I'm meeting Baxter. We're making an igloo."

"Speaking of . . ." Mr. Zakowski tipped the hot scones onto a plate. "I thought he'd be having dinner here the other night. He seemed pretty interested in doing that."

Waylon grabbed his coat from the hook.

"He was hinting pretty hard, buddy. Why didn't you invite him?"

"Dad, we're not, you know . . . friends."

"No? Seems you do a lot of stuff with him."

Waylon felt his stomach roll. He always felt queasy whenever the subject of Baxter and Eddy came up around his parents. Waylon was a terrible liar, and just the thought of trying to hide what he and Baxter were doing made him feel the way he had the last Fourth of July, after a plate of bad fried clams.

"I don't know why you'd want me to be friends with a criminal," he mumbled.

Mr. Zakowski looked up sharply. "What's that supposed to mean?"

"Nothing. I'm just not friends with Baxter. We do stuff together about that dog we visit. Like this igloo—we're making it so we can visit with him there." Waylon pressed his lips together so they wouldn't say anything more and jammed his hands into his gloves. "I have to go, Dad."

Mr. Zakowski heaved a sigh that said *All*

right, but think about it, then slid four scones into a paper bag and tucked it inside Waylon's jacket. "Two for you; two for your not-friend," he said. "And keep your hood up—it's cold out there."

Waylon stopped at his condo's storage area for a shovel, and then pushed open the back door. Plowing through the sparkling drifts, the scones warm against his chest, he did think about what his dad had said.

Sometimes Waylon thought that Baxter would make a good friend. Baxter always listened whenever Waylon mentioned some fascinating science—he never acted bored, and he never laughed.

He never horned in on Waylon's days with Eddy.

And Baxter was easy to talk to. Waylon's friend Rasheed liked to shoulder-butt people

every few sentences. His cousin Josh broke into monkey hoots when he was excited. Charlie inserted the punch lines of funny movies into everything he said. For the last month, it had been "Holy Kooka-Moly," which Waylon didn't find so hilarious after the first hundred times.

Once in a while, Baxter talked out of the side of his mouth, the way he said detective partners do so criminals can't read their lips. But otherwise he just talked. No shoulder-butts, no monkey hoots, no punch lines. That was a good thing in a friend, wasn't it?

But after thinking like this for a while, Waylon always remembered: Baxter Boylen was the closest thing to a juvenile delinquent he had ever encountered. Almost every day, it seemed, Principal Rice hauled him down to her office. And he had pretty much *become* the *Encyclopedia of Crime* he checked out so often. In the just the past week, Baxter had informed Waylon that leaving the US with more than five dollars in pennies can land you in jail for five years; a person with an identical twin can't be found guilty based on DNA evidence; and the electric chair was invented by a dentist.

He'd dropped these bombshells as though they were nothing, but Waylon had felt himself blanching.

Wasn't it safer to stay away from someone that interested in criminal activity? Who practically lived in the principal's office? Except when it came to Dumpster Eddy, Waylon kept a distance from Baxter Boylen.

He turned the corner, and there was Baxter. Waylon had to admit he didn't look anything like a criminal, smiling and waving a shovel. Still.

Waylon pulled the bag of scones out. "From *my dad*," he said.

5

"Okay," Baxter said, after they'd licked their gloves clean of scone crumbs, one finger at a time. "So, like we decided last night, this is the perfect location. It's exactly in between our homes, so Eddy will know we're nearby and won't run away."

Waylon pointed to the apartment building on their right. "And my friend Mitchell lives there—my parents won't wonder why I'm coming here all the time."

Waylon and Baxter squeezed through a passage to the back alley. The alley had a good, unused look: it had been plowed, but nobody had shoveled out paths from the doorways, and there were no footprints. Large snow-covered mounds might be garbage cans or air-conditioning equipment— an igloo would blend right in.

Waylon pointed to a corner where two brick walls met. A Dumpster guarded the nook from view. "How about back there?" He trudged through the drifts. "I like it," he called to Baxter. "It's already protected on three sides, like a cave."

Baxter scuffed in along the path Waylon had made. He stood and surveyed the space, nodding. "There's supposed to be another storm Saturday night. If we can finish the igloo by then, the new snow will camouflage it." He clumped over to the Dumpster and swept off a spot on its lid. He hoisted himself up and tipped his head toward the space beside him.

Waylon climbed up. From the new perspective, the alley sparkled with promise. He felt a smile lift his face. This was real. He and Baxter would make a secret home here for their dog, Dumpster Eddy.

Their *dog*—Waylon was finally going to own *a dog*. Just sitting on the Dumpster made him feel closer to Eddy.

Maybe he'd give himself a matching nickname. Dumpster Waylon . . . that sounded pretty good.

Although, of course, it would have to be a secret nickname.

Waylon had gotten himself a journal in the fall. In it he'd begun to track his life's work as a scientist. Pretty soon, he planned to send this journal off to Neil deGrasse Tyson.

Neil deGrasse Tyson, he hoped, would be so impressed, he'd invite Waylon to be a junior correspondent on his show. But Neil deGrasse Tyson wouldn't ask someone named Dumpster Waylon to be a junior correspondent, that was for sure. No, Dumpster Waylon would be something he'd only call himself around his dog.

His dog! Waylon glanced over at Baxter. He was surveying the alley with a pleased expression, as if he was feeling the same way Waylon was.

Maybe he would let Baxter call him by the secret nickname, too.

Baxter spread his hands. "Okay, so how do we build it?"

Waylon scooped together a snow pillow and leaned back. The bright blue sky glittered with frosty powder drifting from the rooftops. "An igloo's made of blocks of snow," he began in the voice he would use if he actually did get to be a junior correspondent on Neil deGrasse Tyson's TV show. "First we set a row of big ones in a circle. Then we take a snow saw, and we—"

"A snow saw?"

Waylon nodded, but he saw the problem. "I'm sure we can figure out something else. Anything that will cut through the blocks. We need to take the tops off the first row, slanting up and inward." He held his hand out at an angle and spiraled it up. "After that, the blocks form a dome."

"I don't get it."

Waylon sat up. He tugged off his gloves and dug into his shirt pocket for a pencil. He pulled the empty scone bag from his coat and began to draw. "See? The angle helps the rows support each other."

Baxter nodded. "How about air? How will Eddy breathe?"

"There will be chinks between the blocks—we won't fill in all of them. We'll stick tubes—maybe pieces of hose—through some of them. Horizontally, so that even if it snows again they won't get blocked." Waylon dropped to the ground and scuffed out a circle about six feet across. "This will be the perimeter."

Baxter followed, stamping the circle into a flat ring. "How about a door?"

"Right. There's usually a short tunnel, so the

wind doesn't blow straight in." Waylon moved toward the back wall and dragged an *X* with his boot. "Here, so it's hidden from the alley. Let's start making some blocks."

Baxter scanned the empty alley. "What if this friend of yours sees us building it?"

Waylon shook his head. "Mitchell can keep a secret. Clementine lives in the same building. She wouldn't tell either. Let's get started."

Waylon lifted the Dumpster lid, crumpled the scone bag, and was about to throw it away when Baxter grabbed his sleeve. "Wait. Any crumbs left?"

Waylon passed over the bag and Baxter shook it over his mouth. "Man, those were good. I bet you hope your dad never hears about his screenplay."

"No." Waylon put on his gloves and picked up his shovel. "I really hope he hears soon."

"Oh, right," Baxter said. "Because then he'll be famous, and you guys will be rich!"

Waylon dropped his head. He stabbed his shovel into the snow and cut a square. Then another and another.

Of course he was excited about what his father was doing. Mr. Zakowski used to work at an insurance office. A normal job, not too bad, Waylon had thought. The kind of job with spin-around chairs and a box of doughnuts in the break room—imagine being able to stop in for free doughnuts anytime you felt like it.

But Waylon's father hadn't seen it that way. "That job was crushing the creativity out of me," he explained. So, about a year and a half ago, on June 14, his fortieth birthday, he'd quit. Snapped his laptop shut, unpinned Waylon's and Neon's art from his cubicle walls and swept it into his briefcase. He'd yanked off his necktie and tossed it into a box of doughnuts on his way out, whistling "Oh Happy Day."

Waylon liked imagining the scene—it made him proud to have a father who'd done something so dramatic. And it was pretty thrilling to think that one day he and his family and all his friends, and oh yes, *the whole world, including Neil deGrasse Tyson*, would go into a theater and watch a movie his own father had scripted.

But in his secret heart of hearts, Waylon was also a teeny, tiny bit worried. What if . . . ?

"What if it doesn't work?"

Waylon spun around. "Of course it will work! Wait. What?"

Baxter pointed to the dozens of squares Waylon had carved into the surface. "I think the snow's too fluffy. How are you going to get those out as blocks?"

Waylon slid his shovel under a square and

lifted. The snow crumbled into a pile of pow-der.

"I've got an idea." Baxter plowed back to the Dumpster.

Waylon leaned on his shovel, thinking about his father again.

Two years, was the deal Mr. Zakowski had made with the family. For two years, he would take odd jobs on the weekends, but otherwise he was just going to write. If he hadn't sold a script by the end of those two years, he'd go back to crunching numbers. Every time he promised that—"I'll go back to crunching numbers"—he made it sound like *I'll go back to wrestling croco-diles in the sewer.*

June 14 was only five months away.

Baxter came back, holding a shoe box. He packed it with snow, then he turned it over. The block held its shape, only crumbling at the

edges. But when Baxter tried to lift it, it broke
in half. "What we need is some water, to pack
it down harder," he said. "And a box that's not
cardboard."

"We've got a picnic cooler," Waylon remembered.

"Perfect." Baxter ditched his shovel behind

the Dumpster. "Let's go get it. Maybe your dad's making something great for lunch. . . ."

Waylon turned away. "Well, uh . . . it's my day with Eddy," he said. "I want to show him snow. Let's meet here Saturday morning and build it then."

6

When Waylon arrived at the lockup, Eddy knocked him down, licking him all over, as usual. But then he started whining. He sniffed all around Waylon in widening circles. He stood on his hind legs at the lockup door as if he was looking for something.

"Let's go for a walk," Waylon urged. Eddy woofed a final cry at the door and followed Waylon to the Animal Control office.

This time, Officer Sure-Not-Meg just waved

okay without even looking up from his papers. Waylon took the old collar from its hook and fastened it around Eddy's neck. He clipped on the ratty leash Meg kept beside the collar and led Eddy outside.

"Eddy, meet snow," Waylon said. "Snow, meet Eddy."

Dumpster Eddy and snow seemed to be old friends. Eddy zigzagged across the sidewalk,

scrambling up and down the shoveled mounds. He plunged and rolled and shook himself off, plunged and rolled and shook himself off.

In the dog park, Waylon let him off the leash. He took an apple from his pocket and threw it. "Fetch!"

Eddy looked puzzled for a minute. Then he tunneled into the snow near where the apple had disappeared. Eventually he popped up, whuffling snow from his snout, the apple in his mouth. He trotted back and handed it over.

Waylon threw the apple again. This time, Eddy dove in a couple of feet past where it had entered the snow and retrieved it perfectly.

"Wow. Genius dog."

Waylon looked up. A teenage girl stood beside him. She wore a red scarf wound around her face so he could only see her eyes. They were watching Eddy in wonder.

"He is," Waylon agreed. He tossed the apple again. "He's figuring the apple's trajectory."

"He's like the Einstein of dogs," the girl said. Puffs of steam leaked out of her scarf with the words. "You're so lucky." Then she ducked her head deeper into her scarf and moved on down the path.

"I am," Waylon said out loud. "I am so lucky." He swept a bench clear of snow and sat down to watch his dog.

He had to admit that Dumpster Eddy wasn't much to look at. In fact, Eddy struck him as the kind of thing that would happen if some aliens decided to make an Earth dog, and they understood the basics—four legs on the bottom, a head on one end and a tail at the other—but all they had was a pile of leftover parts. The kind of parts that actual Earth dogs would have rejected as being too ugly.

Waylon loved this mismatched dog with all his heart, which, whenever he saw Eddy, he could feel swelling so fast it seemed in danger of exploding right out of his chest.

For as long as he could remember, a dog had been the one thing missing from his life. Not a cat or a bird or even a potbellied pig, which his mother had offered once, since it didn't have fur for her to be allergic to.

No, it had always been a dog and only a dog for him.

A year ago, Waylon had started to build himself a robot puppy. He'd filled a stuffed poodle—a realistic one, of course, not some dumb fuzzy toy—with springs and gears and a mini recorder with twelve different barks, all wired to a remote control. He'd programmed the tail to wag and the ears to perk, and he knew that with a few simple parts from his mother's robotics lab he could make that dog roll over and trot and probably even play Frisbee in the park.

But he'd stopped.

He stopped because of the eyes. The robot dog's eyes were dull black, like stones, and they had bothered Waylon.

He'd understood why when he met Dumpster Eddy. Eddy's eyes were shining with life. They could be worried or trusting, joyful or sad, playful or serious. Intelligent eyes. Waylon had known then that no robot dog would ever have understood him—grokked him—the way a real dog could.

The way Dumpster Eddy did.

And he grokked Eddy, too.

Eddy bounded up onto the bench and shook the snow from his coat. Waylon knew he could grok with Eddy right now and find out what the whining in the station had been about. But for some reason he didn't want to.

Eddy shivered. Waylon unzipped his coat and held it open. "Hop in," he invited.

Eddy did, and Waylon zipped him up until only the tip of his nose poked out. He carried him the seven blocks back to the lockup. And even though Dumpster Eddy was twenty-three pounds (Meg had weighed him), nestled against Waylon's chest, he didn't feel any heavier than an extra heart.

7

Friday morning, Charlie was waiting for Waylon in the Pit. He handed over *Cosmo-Quest*, beaming.

Waylon beamed back. He opened the booklet and read. His smile disappeared.

Neil deGrasse Tyson would never take him seriously if he saw something like this.

He held the booklet out. "What's this?" he asked. "Right here. *Astronaut Char-Lon got off the hover-board and slipped on some green slime.*

You changed what I wrote, Charlie! There's no green slime on Pluto. Pluto is covered in reddish dust."

Charlie rolled his eyes. "Reddish dust isn't funny. Green slime is."

"But green slime isn't scientifically accurate. Reddish dust is."

Charlie air-waved Waylon's words away.

"The science has to be right," Waylon said, a little louder than he'd meant to. He was starting to get riled up by the air-waving. "It's an *astrophysics* comic."

Charlie crossed his arms over his chest. "It's an astrophysics *comic*. The funny has to be funny!"

"All right, fine," Charlie grumbled when the first bell rang. "How about this: Astronaut Char-Lon falls into this hole, this hole *in the reddish dust*, and at the bottom—"

"No, that couldn't happen," Waylon interrupted. "He couldn't *fall* in. Not without a gravity suit."

"So what? It would be hilarious! Holy Kooka-Moly!"

"Hilarious, maybe," Waylon admitted, "but it's called *Cosmo-Quest*, not *Made-Up-Stuff Quest*!"

Charlie's face crashed.

"I'm sorry, Charlie, but science is science." Waylon walked into the classroom, disheartened that anyone would want to mess with something as amazing and perfect as science.

All day, he only grew more depressed. He'd pinned a lot of hopes on *Cosmo-Quest*. At the end of school, he slumped into the Pit, avoiding Charlie, who was avoiding him.

Baxter came up to

Waylon during the avoiding. "Can you go with me to see Eddy today?" he asked.

Waylon felt his bad mood completely, instantly evaporate. "Yes!" He pulled out his scientific life's work journal. *Investigate the mood-altering power of dogs*, he wrote, then tucked it back in his pocket. "Yes!" he shouted again, hurrying after Baxter.

"Hey," he said, catching up. "How come you're letting me share your day today?"

"So Eddy will have company. The chief wants to see me in his office again."

Waylon shivered as he walked alongside Baxter. "Are you in trouble?"

"Of course not!" Baxter looked insulted, as if the mere idea were ludicrous.

"Well, you were in trouble with Principal Rice on Wednesday. Clementine said you put guts in her briefcase."

"Guts? No, *nuts*," Baxter said. "I filled it with nuts. It was a total success."

"Except you got caught," Waylon said.

"Don't care. That wasn't the point."

"Then what was?"

Baxter stopped. He looked more serious than Waylon had ever seen him. "I am going to be the world's greatest criminologist when I grow up. To do that, I have to understand how the criminal mind works. To do *that*, I have to re-create their crimes myself."

Waylon got it. He always understood famous experiments better when he repeated them himself. "So what does that have to do with Mrs. Rice?"

"I always try them out on her. On Wednesday, I re-created the Great Ruby Heist of 1989, which used identical briefcases. I'd seen Mrs. Rice's briefcase when I went to her office the day before. I realized there was one exactly like it in the back of my dad's closet. The actual crooks substituted fake rubies, but I only had all these walnuts, left over from Christmas. The point was, I switched her briefcase."

"And Principal Rice lets you get away with this stuff?"

"Not exactly. But she sees I'm fulfilling my destiny."

Waylon appreciated destiny, too. Since he was little, he'd known it was his destiny to be a scientist. "Sure, okay," he said. "Still, I can't believe you don't get detention."

"Oh, I do. I owe a total of thirty-eight hours now. But Mrs. Rice knows I'm studying to become a junior police officer. She says if I earn my certificate, she'll wipe out all the detentions."

"Wow. I didn't know she was so nice."

Baxter smacked his forehead. "Here's the weird part. She says she's not being nice! She says she's doing it because when she retires, she figures she's going to need a friend on the police department."

"You're making that up," Waylon said. "She's the principal of the whole school!"

Baxter shrugged. "Think about it. You spend all those years making rules, and forcing kids to follow rules, and punishing kids for not following rules . . . well, I bet it makes you want to break some rules sometimes."

Waylon brushed the idea away. Baxter was messing with him. "So if you're not in trouble, how come you're seeing the chief today?"

"He's helping me study for the junior-officer course." Baxter pulled a pamphlet from his jacket. "Today he's testing me on Traits of the Ideal Police Officer. You can quiz me on the way."

Waylon took the pamphlet and they started out again. "Okay, what's number seven?"

"Hmmm. Is that about teamwork?"

"Yep."

"Okay . . . *A good officer demonstrates the ability to work on a team. A good officer values the different and unique skills of others.*"

"Perfect," Waylon said. "How about number three?"

Baxter slid on a patch of icy sidewalk and then rebalanced. "Number three. Respect for

Individuals. *A good officer demonstrates an ability to work with people of various backgrounds, beliefs, and opinions."*

Right down the list, Baxter didn't miss a single trait. Protects a Source, Perseveres, Has a Partner's Back, Shows Good Community Morals—Baxter knew them all.

By the time they got to the station, Waylon had learned a whole lot about police officers, too.

But not as much as he'd learned about Baxter Boylen.

Seeing Eddy four days in a row was great. But as he said good-bye and latched the cage, Waylon realized how much he wished he could have Eddy full-time. He was still feeling sad when he walked into the kitchen.

"Apple-cranberry," Mr. Zakowski said,

waving his hand over a pie on the counter.
"Spun caramel topping. Extremely tricky. How
was your afternoon?"

Waylon dropped his backpack and slumped
onto a stool. "Good and bad. That dog? He's
back. I took him for a walk. That was the
good."

"He's back again? Seems he's there a lot."

Waylon felt his stomach flip. "Um . . . he's a repeat offender." He pointed to the pie. "So, no word yet?"

"No word yet. Must be nice for you, having that dog around. Almost like having your own, eh?"

Waylon sighed. "Almost. Except not."

"So what was the bad today?"

Waylon pulled *Cosmo-Quest* out of his pack and handed it over. "I got it back from Charlie." He dropped his head to the counter. "It's ruined. Charlie changed what I wrote. He didn't care about the science."

Mr. Zakowski sat down. "Collaboration's tricky," he said. "You can't disrespect someone else's skills."

Waylon swallowed hard. Was his dad talking about Charlie, or him?

Mr. Zakowski reached over and grabbed two forks from a drawer. He pulled the pie between them. "Pie's famous for cheering people up. Let's see if it works."

Waylon stuck in his fork and took a bite. It was delicious. But it didn't work.

8

"Your dad left early," Waylon's mother said when he came into the kitchen Saturday morning. "He's setting up the lights for a show at the Beantown Rep. He said you could join him at the theater if you want."

"No, thanks." Waylon fixed a bowl of cereal and sat down. After a few bites, he noticed his mom was dressed in her lab clothes instead of her Saturday sweatpants. He pointed his spoon at her hair, which was pinned in a tight going-to-work bun. "What's up?"

Mrs. Zakowski flashed an excited smile. "Boston General is sending a team of neuro-surgeons over to the lab this morning. They want to see my new robotics model. Want to come along, watch the presentation?"

Hearing the words *neurosurgeons* and *new robotics model* in the same sentence was almost too much to resist. Almost.

"I can't." Waylon bent over his cereal again, hoping his mother wouldn't ask why.

Mrs. Zakowski sat beside him and pressed her hand to his forehead. "Are you feeling okay?"

"I'm fine. I just have something to do this morning."

Waylon's mother cocked her head, frowning. "No to the Rep? No to the lab? Must be something important."

Waylon kept his gaze on his cornflakes as he answered. "I'm building an igloo. With Baxter."

"That sounds like fun," his mother said. "For a fort?"

Waylon would have to work hard to only let out a little bit of the truth. "No. It's for . . . You know that dog Baxter and I take for walks sometimes? He's back, and we thought we could play with him there."

"The same dog? How does he keep getting loose?"

"Uh . . ." The cereal sloshed in Waylon's stomach. He pushed the bowl away. "Can I borrow a cooler to make the snow blocks with?"

Mrs. Zakowski went into the pantry and came back a minute later carrying two coolers, a big one and a small one. "Honey, I'm sorry."

"About what? These are great."

"No, I mean . . . I'm sorry you can't have

a dog. I've never seen anyone want one more, and it breaks my heart that I'm the reason you can't have one."

Waylon jumped up to throw his arms around his mother. "It's not your fault." He forced a smile. "Besides, when I'm a famous scientist, I'll invent an anti-dog-allergy pill, and you won't be allergic anymore!"

Mrs. Zakowski laughed and scrubbed his head. "If anyone can do that, kiddo, it's going to be you. Now get out of here."

* * *

Baxter showed up carrying two plastic bowls. "One for water, one for food," he said.

Waylon held up the wicker basket he'd found in his building's laundry room. "His bed."

"Also this." Baxter pulled a flashlight out of his pack. "It's going to be dark in there."

"Actually, it won't be that dark," Waylon said. "Snow is pretty translucent."

"Translucent?"

"Look." Waylon held up his hand. "You can't see through it, right? But hold your flashlight against my palm."

Baxter did, and Waylon's hand glowed orange, his bones darker lines. "That's translucence. Even solid things, like . . ."—Waylon pointed to the building—"like even those brick walls allow some light through. Our eyes just can't detect it."

Baxter didn't look convinced.

91

"Really," Waylon said. "Twenty percent of the light that hits the igloo will make it through. Eddy will be able to see well enough, at least during the daytime."

"Well, we'll find out when it's finished." Baxter took the lids off the coolers. "Let's get started. Do we have water?"

"I called Mitchell. He said he'll bring some down to his lobby at ten."

When they walked into Mitchell's building, they found Clementine taping snowflakes to a window in the lobby. Mitchell stepped out of the elevator, holding four plastic jugs of water.

"Yo, Science Dude," Mitchell said.

"Yo, Science Dude," Waylon said back. Sometimes Waylon automatically repeated whatever Mitchell said. This was because Mitchell was fourteen and a sports star. "I mean, yo, Mitchell."

Clementine dropped her tape. "What are you

doing here, Waylon?" she demanded. "Baseball is over."

Mitchell set the jugs on the floor and clapped his hands to his chest as though he'd been stabbed. "Dudette, baseball is *never* over," he corrected her. "It's *eternal*."

Waylon's hands clapped themselves over his chest. "It's *eternal*," he repeated. "It's *never* over."

"Well, Mitchell's not teaching you how to play today," Clementine said, pointing out the window at the piles of snow. "So what are you doing? What's the water for?"

"Nothing," Baxter said before Waylon could answer. He picked up the jugs and headed for the doors. Their supply sled awaited them outside.

They got to work right away: shoveling snow into the coolers, sprinkling it with water, and packing it down. Then they overturned each block to harden in the freezing air. When they had enough bigger ones for the first row, they laid them around the perimeter, tight against each other.

"I forgot about a snow saw," Waylon admitted. "You?"

Baxter drew a coil of wire from his pocket. "Ta-da!"

"What will that do?" Waylon asked.

"What *won't* it do is the question." Baxter looked smug. "'Metal wire is the most valuable tool in the criminal's arsenal,'" he said, and Waylon could tell he was reciting from the *Encyclopedia of Crime*. "'It can be used to jimmy locks, rewire alarms, tie up kidnapping victims, break into cars, slice through—'"

"Okay, okay," Waylon interrupted. "How's it supposed to cut snow blocks?"

"Watch and learn," Baxter said. He unrolled

about two feet of wire and held it taut. "Angled like this?" he asked.

Waylon nodded. Baxter sliced the wire through the block. When Waylon lifted off the top of the block, what was left was slanted just right.

Baxter cut through the next block and the next, all around the entire first row. When they set the second row, the blocks leaned in just the way Waylon had predicted.

They worked steadily through the morning, making blocks and stacking them. The igloo walls were about waist-high when they heard the sound of laughter.

"Uh-oh." Baxter pointed down the alley. Clementine was towing a little kid on a sled. "What if she sees us?"

"She'll ask a million questions, that's all," Waylon said. "I'll out-question her until she gives up."

Clementine drew up. The little boy on the sled tumbled off and began filling his hat with snow.

"What are you doing?" Clementine asked.

"Building an igloo. What's your brother's name today?"

"Arugula. How come you're building an igloo?"

"It's for that dog I told you about. Remember?"

"Oh, so it's a dogloo," Clementine decided. "How are you going to keep him warm?"

"Snow is good insulation," Waylon said. "Is *dogloo* a real word?"

Clementine shrugged, and then she grimaced. "I sure wouldn't let my cat live in an ice house. Even if you called it a catloo."

"Of course not. Cats are desert animals," Waylon told her, remembering a *Miracles of the Natural World* episode he'd seen. "Did you know they come from Egypt?"

"I know that," Clementine said. "The Egyptians used to embalm them into tiny mummies when they died."

"Well, did you know that the scientific term for a hair ball is *bezoar*?" Waylon asked.

Clementine frowned. "No, I didn't. Did you know that most male cats are left-pawed?"

"Nope," Waylon admitted. "Did you know that the world's most expensive coffee comes from Indonesia? Wild cats there eat the coffee berries and poop them out. Apparently it makes the coffee delicious."

"Seriously?" Clementine asked.

Waylon crossed his heart.

Clementine's eyes widened. She plopped her brother onto the sled and grabbed the handle. "I have to go," she called over her shoulder as she ran off. "My dad's making coffee."

9

Nobody bothered them for the rest of the morning, and the dogloo grew quickly. Nearing the top, they used the smaller blocks and the rows grew smaller, too, until there was only a pizza-size space left in the roof.

"Do we leave it open?" Baxter asked.

"Not always. Too much heat would escape," Waylon explained. "The last block fits in like a cork: wider at the top, so it doesn't fall in."

Baxter and Waylon rolled a big snowball,

packed it down tight, and then shaved off the sides. Together they lifted it into place.

Then they stepped back. Just a few hours before, there had been nothing on the ground behind the Dumpster. Now there was a whole doghouse made of snow, perfectly round and smooth and gleaming white.

"I don't know," Baxter said, rubbing his chin. "Something's missing."

"No," Waylon said. "I researched it. We did everything right. The only thing left is the tunnel entrance."

Baxter shook his head slowly, studying the igloo. "It's too blank or something."

"It's made of snow," Waylon said. "You can't get blanker than that. Let's make the entrance."

The tunnel was short, and since they were experienced igloo builders now, it wasn't long before they placed the final blocks.

Baxter stood back and squinted. "I still think it's missing something, but I can't figure out what." He stacked the coolers and water jugs onto the sled. "Did your dad sell his screenplay?"

Waylon shook his head. "No. But he will. It's a thramedy. That's a thriller, a drama, and a comedy all in one. It's going to be a blockbuster."

"Cool! What's it about?"

"Uh . . . actually . . ."

"Don't worry," Baxter said from the corner of his mouth, "I won't tell."

"It's not that. It's that . . . I haven't read it."

"What? How come?"

Waylon picked up his shovel. "I don't know," he said, surprised to find that he really didn't. "Let's clear a path to the alley."

Just then, Clementine appeared again. She blocked their way until they looked up.

"My mother is a really big fan of fresh air," she said, shaking her head dramatically. "She drags my poor baby sister outside every day, no matter what. And Summer doesn't even have any hair yet—just a little fuzz! This winter's gotten so cold, my dad bought a heating pad for—"

"Your mother leaves a baby outside in winter?" Waylon asked. "She should at least build her an igloo."

"I might have to turn her in," Baxter warned. "That might be a jailable offense."

"Of course not!" Clementine cried. "You guys aren't listening. My dad bought a *heating pad* for her stroller. You could—"

"Great." Baxter cut her off. "That's super-great for your sister, but so what?" He started shoveling again.

"Sorry, Clementine," Waylon said. "We still have work to do."

Clementine rolled her eyes. "Boys!" she muttered.

Waylon leaned on his shovel and watched her stomp away to her building. He could tell she wished the snow wasn't muffling her stomping—she looked pretty mad. Which he didn't understand. "Girls," he muttered.

"Girls," Baxter echoed. "Back to work."

But before they'd cleared another dozen feet, Clementine returned.

She held out a yellow-striped flannel pad about the size of a cookie sheet. *"Feel* it. *Both* of you," she ordered. "It's *warm.* It's for *outside.* It runs on a *battery.* For *outside heating!"*

Waylon and Baxter dropped their shovels as it dawned on them.

"This will be perfect!" Baxter shouted.

"Thanks, Clementine!" Waylon reached for the pad.

Clementine yanked it away. "You can't *have* it, of course! I just told you, it's for my *sister!*"

Waylon and Baxter looked at each other and shook their heads. They picked up their shovels again.

"You guys are missing the point!"

When they looked up, Clementine shook the stroller pad at them. "If my dad could buy one, so could you."

All evening, Waylon found himself wondering about what Baxter had asked. Why had he never read his father's screenplay?

After dinner, he knocked on his sister's door.

"Entre!" ordered a bored voice from inside.

Waylon's sister was the opposite of Waylon. Whereas Waylon had known from the day he was born who he was—a scientist—Charlotte was a tryer-onner. Last year she'd tried on a new name, Neon, a new wardrobe of tattered all-black clothes, and an attitude to match. This semester she was taking French, so she'd been trying on a French twist to her personality.

"Entre!" she called again, and Waylon stepped inside.

"Neon, have you read *Collision Course?*"

Neon pinched the bridge of her nose and frowned as though the thoughts she was thinking were so deep they hurt. *"Non,"* she admitted at last.

Waylon cut his eyes in the direction of their father's studio.

"Oui," Neon agreed, rising from her chair. "Perhaps it is *ze* time."

They found their father at his desk. He closed his email. "No news," he reported.

"Dad, could we read it?" Waylon asked. "Your screenplay?"

Mr. Zakowski looked pleased. "Well, sure," he said. "It's pretty grown-up stuff, but I think you two can handle it." He lifted a stack of papers and handed it over. He stood up. "I'm running the lights at the Rep tonight," he said. "I'll be back in a couple of hours."

Waylon and Neon flopped onto the floor, the stack between them. As they read the first page, Waylon noticed how silent the room was.

Page after page, the silence grew deeper.

Waylon stole a glance at his sister. "Something big is going to happen soon," he predicted, trying to sound certain. "It's a thramedy, remember?"

Neon nodded hopefully.

More reading. More not-laughing, more not-gasping-in-suspense, more . . . silence.

Waylon held up a page. "There's kissing on this one," he said. It sounded lame, even to his own ears, as if he were apologizing.

"Actually," Neon said, looking more closely, "there's just some talking about kissing. And then some talking about not kissing."

After a few minutes, Waylon pointed. "Duke gets up out of his chair here. See? *He jumps up from his chair.*"

"Oh, *oui*," Neon agreed. Then she tapped the bottom of the page. "*Duke sits back down again*," she read.

An hour later, Waylon stretched. "Neon, nothing happens in this thing."

Just then, Mr. Zakowski stuck his head in the door. "Well, guys? What do you think?" he asked with a smile, spreading his hands over the papers on the floor.

Neon tugged her beret over one eye. "I think

I have to go to bed. Au revoir," she said, slinking out of the room.

Mr. Zakowski turned to Waylon.

"Um . . . I think you forgot to give us the pages with the good parts, Dad. The parts with stuff happening."

"What do you mean? That screenplay is packed with stuff happening."

"No, I mean *interesting* stuff. Isn't this supposed to be a thriller?"

"It is." Mr. Zakowski bent over and rifled through the pages. "Here, listen to this line: *Stand aside. Let me fulfill my destiny!* Now that's called thrilling, Waylon!"

"No, Dad! That's called talking. Things exploding are thrilling. The title is *Collision Course*—where are the collisions?"

"The title is about destiny, Waylon. People's

destinies, on a collision course with each other."

Waylon felt the air leave his body. Or maybe it was hope, gasping au revoir.

10

Sunday morning, the world looked fresh and hopeful again, frosted with an inch of new snow during the night.

Waylon met Baxter in front of Baby Goods. Baxter pulled a wad of bills out of his pocket and handed it over. Waylon emptied his wallet and counted everything. "Fifty-eight dollars and fifty cents."

Baxter whistled. "A fortune," he said from

the corner of his mouth. "Eddy deserves it." He reached for the door.

"Wait," Waylon said. "What if someone asks why two kids are buying a stroller pad?"

Baxter shrugged. "So what if they do?"

Waylon hung his head. "I'll wreck everything. I'll blurt out that it's for a dog. And next thing you know, I'll spill the beans about how we're busting Eddy out, and we'll probably both end up in jail."

Baxter stared at Waylon. "Why would you do that?"

Waylon pulled Baxter out of the doorway. "I have this book, *The Science of Being Human*. The Body Language chapter lists the things people do when they're lying."

"What kind of stuff?"

"Well, there's . . . Opposite Nodding," Waylon said. "Like, if you say *no* and that's a lie, you'll automatically nod your head yes."

"Huh. Well, don't do that." Baxter stepped up to the door again.

Waylon grabbed his coat sleeve. "Also, there's Freezing. People who are lying tend to not move, like an animal frozen in fear. And there's Rogatory Position—that's speaking with your palms up." Waylon turned his hands over. "See? It's as if I'm praying for you to believe me. Dead giveaway."

"So this is great," Baxter said. "You know all the things not to do. Let's go in."

Waylon shook his head. "Knowing all this stuff works the opposite way for me. If I even think about lying, somehow I start doing all these things. Plus I feel sick."

Baxter grabbed the door handle. "Fine. You stay outside. I'll go buy it."

Waylon handed over the wallet, but as soon

as Baxter disappeared, he realized he didn't want to be left behind. He wanted to be part of everything to do with Dumpster Eddy, especially the important things, like keeping him warm.

He hurried inside and caught up with Baxter. "I'll let you do all the talking," he promised.

They found the heating pad on the third aisle. Yellow and white stripes, looking warm even in its plastic wrap. Below it was a price tag: $74.99.

Baxter patted his pockets, as if maybe he'd left some money behind, and shook his head. Waylon took the wallet and counted their money again. He shook his head, too.

Baxter picked up the pad. "Remember, you don't say a word," he side-mouthed as they reached the checkout.

The woman behind the counter looked like the kind of grandmother you saw in picture books. The kind who sat in rocking chairs knitting and called you *dearie*. Waylon thought this was a good sign.

Baxter thumped the heating pad onto the counter. "This one's too much money," he said. "Do you have one that's less? Like, fifty-eight dollars and fifty cents?"

The grandmothery lady made a sad face. "That's our only model, I'm afraid. It's very popular."

Baxter sighed and left to put the heating pad back.

"Well, I think I've seen everything now!" The grandmothery woman leaned over the counter to smile at Waylon. "Two fine young gentlemen, wanting to buy their baby brother or sister a nice cuddly heating pad. What's your little one's name?"

Waylon's throat went dry. "Ah . . . we call him Dumpster Eddy."

"Dumpster Eddy? Oh . . . well, how old is he?"

Waylon knew he should lie. But he felt his stomach lurching and his body freezing and his palms floating into Rogatory Position, so he stuck with the truth. "We don't really know. He's about this high." He forced his palm down to Eddy height. "When his ears are perked up."

The grandmothery lady looked confused. "Well, I'll bet he's cute. Do you have a picture?"

Waylon did. Before he could pull out his wallet, Baxter tore up the aisle and stomped on his foot.

"He *is* cute," Baxter said. "Big brown eyes. We have to go now." He grabbed Waylon's sleeve and dragged him outside. "You really *can't* lie!" he said, shaking his head. "So, wait. You never told your parents about busting out Eddy, did you? That was a secret."

"No. But it's just because they never asked."

"Lucky thing," Baxter said.

Except Waylon didn't feel lucky. He turned away. And right across the street was something that actually *did* make him feel lucky. "A pet-supply store!"

When the traffic light turned green, he

and Baxter hurried across. Inside, everything smelled like owning a pet. It smelled like happiness. Waylon and Baxter wandered the aisles for half an hour, weighing their options.

The problem was money. Fifty-eight dollars and fifty cents wasn't a fortune after all.

"Just the basics," Waylon said. "Just what he really, really needs."

When they brought their cart to the checkout, it held a shiny red collar, a retractable leash, and a case of dog food. Waylon dumped their money on the counter.

"Want a name tag for that collar? Only a buck." The cashier pointed to a bowl of round white disks. "You slip it onto the collar. Next to the license tag."

"His license tag?" Waylon asked.

"That they gave you when you got his license."

Waylon and Baxter looked at each other. Then they looked at the floor. "Um, we're getting our dog tomorrow," Waylon said.

"Well then, tomorrow you'll need to get a license. Go to City Hall, next to the police station. Twenty bucks."

"Do we have to?" Baxter asked.

The cashier nodded. "It's the law. Besides, you'll want to. If your dog ever gets lost, whoever finds him can call the phone number on his tag."

Twenty dollars for a license. Waylon and Baxter surveyed the cart. They needed the food. They ran their hands over the fancy red collar and the leash that would let Eddy run farther. The twenty-dollar collar and the twenty-dollar leash.

The cashier sighed. "Cut off the end of a belt you don't wear anymore. Poke a few extra holes in it. There's your collar. You need that license."

"Thanks, mister." Waylon slipped a twenty back into in his wallet. The cashier packed the leash and the dog food into a bag, then dropped in a rawhide chew with a wink.

Waylon and Baxter hurried to the dogloo to stash the new stuff. They stacked the cans in a pile, with the rawhide chew on top. Waylon was about to tuck the leash under the bed when Baxter stopped him. "Let's go visit Eddy together today and try it out."

For a minute, Waylon felt the urge to say, *No, we should save all this stuff for tomorrow, when we own him for sure.* But then he realized that was silly. "Okay," he said instead. Because what harm could it possibly do?

11

When they walked into the lockup, Eddy went crazy, as usual. Baxter opened his pen, and Eddy rocketed between the boys, ramping up and down their chests like a skateboarder to slurp their chins.

Dumpster Eddy didn't whine once, Waylon noticed, then pushed the thought away.

Sure-Not-Meg came out of his office then. "That dog has been going crazy since noon." He held out the beat-up collar and ratty leash.

Waylon took the collar but left the leash. He held up the new one, smiling with pride.

"You bought him a leash?"

Waylon nodded. "It's retractable. Eddy can run pretty far on it."

"You bought an expensive leash like that for a mutt you don't own?"

Waylon froze.

"For a mutt who's leaving in two days?"

Baxter slipped the collar over Eddy's neck and snapped on the leash. "We'll have him back at six," he called, dragging Waylon to the door.

Outside, the boys looked at each other. "Do you think he suspects?" Waylon whispered. "I think he suspects."

"Maybe. Don't worry. We'll get Eddy out tomorrow, and then it won't matter what he suspects, because we'll own him. With a license."

Baxter was right. But the anxious feeling

didn't leave Waylon as they walked to the park. Baxter looked worried, too.

Eddy, at least, was delirious. He practically danced down the street, stopping to say hello to anyone who gave him the slightest opportunity, and prancing right into Boston Common as if he owned the whole thing.

Waylon had never seen a dog so happy. It made him feel happy, too. But also a little sad.

"What's wrong?" Baxter asked.

"Nothing. Well . . . it's just . . . I think Eddy likes you more than he likes me," Waylon admitted.

"That's nuts. Why do you think that?"

129

"When I have him, he has a good time, sure. But not like this. He whines a lot, as if something's bothering him. Today—no whining."

"Huh," Baxter said. "I've noticed that, too, when I take him out. He's always sniffing around and whimpering, as if he's lost something."

"Really? He does that with you, too?" And suddenly Waylon understood. "He's like Willy and Lilly!" he cried.

"What?"

"Willy and Lilly's mom and dad got divorced in the summer. They wanted the weekends to be 'one parent, one kid' time, but Lilly and Willy didn't. So they act all whiny unless *both* parents take them out together. Eddy is like them: if one of us takes him out without the other, he's not happy. You and I are like Willy and Lilly's parents."

"No, we're not," Baxter scoffed. "We aren't married!"

Waylon rolled his eyes. "I know that! But still, that's what Eddy's doing. He wants us to take him out *together*."

Just then, Dumpster Eddy shot past them in a spray of snow. He ran just to the end of his twenty-five-foot line, then spun in midair and shot back in the other direction.

"Genius dog," Baxter said. "He's already figured how to get the longest dash."

Waylon watched for a while. It was great to see Eddy run like that. But it worried him, too. "When we're at school, he'll leave the igloo and go running."

"I know. We'll worry about him being in traffic. And being cold, too."

"And getting wet when it rains."

And then they were quiet. Keeping a dog in

an igloo wasn't perfect. It was just the best they could do.

When Waylon got home, his mother was vacuuming the living room, and the rest of the family was in the kitchen, doing their weekend chores. Waylon took out the trash, then came back and put a new liner in the can.

Mr. Zakowski picked up a clutter of papers on the counter. "Look, you had mail yesterday, Charlotte," he said, holding out an envelope. "You didn't open it."

Waylon didn't know why his father looked surprised. Neon didn't do much of *anything* these days except lock herself in her room and work furiously on what she called her *Oeuvre*, which was some sort of performance masterpiece Waylon didn't understand, no matter how many times Neon explained it.

"You didn't open it," Waylon's dad said again. "It's from the Beantown Repertory Theater."

Neon rolled her eyes. "What is *ze* point?" she muttered. But after she'd unloaded the dishwasher, she picked up the envelope, slit the seal, and began to read.

The bored look evaporated. Her eyes bugged open. "I won!" she said. "Third prize! In the New Voices in Boston Theater contest."

"I didn't know you'd entered that," Mr. Zakowski said.

Neon shook her head. "I didn't. Mrs. Tobasco entered me."

"Mrs. Tobasco?" Mrs. Zakowski asked, coming into the kitchen and shutting off the vacuum. "Your algebra teacher?"

Neon nodded, still looking dazed. "She caught me working on my *Oeuvre* in class last month. When she handed it back, she gave me two choices: detention for the rest of the year, or let her submit it to the contest. So, obviously, I let her."

"What's the prize?" Waylon asked. "Is it seventy-five dollars?"

Neon read the letter again. "'Pleased to

inform . . .' blah, blah, blah . . . blah, blah, 'fresh vision . . .' Oh, here it is! 'We have arranged for the theater to be available for a production of your entry.' One night in the middle of June. For the week before, I can use the theater for rehearsals and making scenery."

Both parents hugged their daughter hard. "A real performance at the Beantown Rep!" Mr. Zakowski cried. "I'm so proud of you!"

Mr. Zakowski looked as happy as if he'd won the prize himself. But later, in his room, Waylon wondered: At the exact time he was waiting to hear if his own writing would ever be performed in front of an audience, his kid gets this prize. Did he feel a little bit jealous?

Waylon sat up. His father was running the lights again tonight. He wouldn't be home for another hour. That gave Waylon just enough time to do what needed to be done. He climbed out of bed and padded down the hall and into his father's writing room.

12

"Science!" Waylon growled Monday morning in the Pit.

"Humor!" Charlie growled back, and then left.

"What was that about?" Baxter asked, coming in.

Waylon took *Cosmo-Quest* out of his backpack and handed it over. "It's a comic book Charlie and I are working on. *Were* working on. Until Charlie wrecked it."

Baxter opened the booklet. He flipped through a few pages, chuckling. He laughed out loud. "It's good," he said. "So what's wrong?"

"What's wrong is Charlie changed the science when he put in the jokes. It's ruined."

Baxter looked at the comic again. "But without these jokes, it's just a guy stepping onto a planet."

"Technically, Pluto hasn't been considered a planet since 2006," Waylon corrected him. "It's a dwarf—"

"I don't care," Baxter interrupted. "Without those jokes, you might as well call it *Cosmo-Snooze*."

"Fine," Waylon grumbled. "I'll put in some jokes myself. I'm not going to let Charlie touch it again."

"Well, can you be funny?" Baxter asked.

"Of course! How about this: Two atoms are

walking down the street. One says, 'Uh-oh, I think I lost an electron.' The second atom says, 'Are you sure?' And the first atom says, 'I'm positive!'"

Baxter looked at Waylon blankly. The bell rang. Baxter still stared.

"That's funny," Waylon explained. "When an atom loses an electron, it becomes positive. So what do you think?"

"I think you should Demonstrate the Ability to Work on a Team with People of Various Backgrounds, Beliefs, and Opinions," Baxter said. "You need to Respect the Different and Unique Skills of Charlie. Because you're not funny."

The second bell rang and Mrs. Fernman herded them into the classroom.

Waylon took his seat. Of course he was funny. Maybe that hadn't been his best joke, but he had lots of others.

Anyway, he wasn't going to let *Cosmo-Quest* ruin this day. Later this afternoon, he and Baxter were going to spring Dumpster Eddy for the final time. They were going to own a dog. Not just any dog, but the best dog in the world.

The clock always tortured Waylon on days

he was waiting to see Eddy, but this morning was worse than ever. The second hand dragged as though it were slogging through tar, the minute hand moved like a centipede with concrete shoes, and the hour hand seemed nailed in place.

Time, Einstein had explained, was relative. But he had been talking about factors like distance and velocity. This phenomenon, Waylon thought, was something else. When Mrs. Fernman turned her back, Waylon drew out his notebook. *Harness dog-love powers to slow time,* he wrote.

Finally, the minute hand gave its last lurch to noon, and twenty-nine kids clattered up and into the lunch line. Waylon bumped his way toward the back. "Okay, get this," he said when he got to Baxter. "What do you call a planet that's off its orbit?"

Just then, Principal Rice came to the door.

She crooked her finger at Baxter. He threw up his hands, but he followed her out.

In the lunchroom, Waylon dropped his tray next to Clementine's. "Do you think I'm funny?" he asked.

"You? Funny?" Clementine repeated. "No. But don't worry— you're interesting. That's good, too. So, did you buy one? A heating pad for that dog?"

Waylon slumped onto the lunch table. He felt his cheek bond to decades of apple juice and meat loaf crust, but he didn't care. It was supposed to get really cold tonight.

"No," he admitted. "It costs seventy-five dollars. We're going to save our allowances. Maybe in a month." He sat up. "It's the only thing we don't have. We got him everything else."

He watched as Clementine stuck her straw into her milk and blew up a bubble storm. "Poor dog," she said at last, shaking her head. "That's a *lo-o-o-o-ng, c-o-o-o-o-ld* time."

Waylon pushed away his tray. None of the food on his plate was going to make it past the lump that had grown in his throat.

Baxter's final police test was right after school Monday afternoon. He met Waylon at the dogloo afterward, grinning.

"You passed?" Waylon asked.

"Aced every section. I'm getting my certificate Wednesday afternoon. In a ceremony." He pulled a can opener from his pack and placed it beside the case of food. Then he filled the water dish from his thermos.

Waylon pushed the laundry basket bed to the far edge. "I read that dogs like to feel protected when they sleep," he explained. He fluffed the old blanket he'd brought over the bed, then laid his flannel beagle pajamas on top. "And I cut up a belt for a collar—it's in my pocket."

Baxter scooped out a niche in the wall and wedged the flashlight in so it shone down over everything they'd done. "All we need now is the license," he said. "Let's go."

Just as they crawled out, they saw a pair of green boots in the tunnel entrance.

It was Clementine. She unzipped her jacket,

pulled out the yellow-striped stroller pad, and held it out over both her palms.

Waylon looked up, puzzled.

"Only at night!" Clementine growled. "My mom only takes Summer out in the afternoons, so I'll leave it outside every night. See there?" She aimed a shoulder at her building. "That's

the basement door. Put it back there every morning before school."

"Okay, okay. Thanks!" Waylon reached for the pad, but Clementine yanked it back.

"And it better be clean! Put something over it, so it's not all fleas and dog hair."

"Okay, I promise!" Waylon reached again.

But again Clementine pulled it back. "And it's only until you can buy your own, so hurry up with getting the money!"

"Right, we will!" Baxter promised.

"And one last thing. You can never tell. Anyone."

"We won't."

"I *mean* it. Blood-swear."

Waylon said okay to blood-swearing, although he didn't know what it meant, and finally Clementine handed over the heating pad. Warm in his hands, he could imagine Eddy curling up on it with a smile on his dog-face. "How come you're doing this for us?" he asked.

Clementine shook her head. "I'm not doing it for you."

"Then how come?"

Waylon was shocked at what happened next: Clementine's chin started to quake, and her eyes filled with tears. He knew that everybody cried, from *The Science of Being Human*, Chapter Seven, "People Plumbing." But he'd never seen it happen to Clementine, not even when Mrs. Fernman sent her to the principal's office for something she didn't do.

She wiped her face and looked down the alley. "Last winter, my kitten got lost," she said in a wavery voice. "I worried all the time that he was cold. I don't want to have to worry the same thing about your dog." Then she spun around and stomped back to her building.

Waylon dove into the igloo before Clementine could change her mind. He tucked the pad under the blanket and smoothed it out. Then he spread his pajamas over the top again. He sat back on his heels. Everything was ready now.

He backed outside and stood next to Baxter. For a minute, they both just took it all in.

"OAT," Waylon said after a while.

"What?" Baxter asked.

Waylon hadn't realized he'd spoken out loud. "OAT," he said. "When I was little, I made up this game called OAT—One Awesome Thing. I made everyone say One Awesome Thing about the day. This dogloo is my OAT today."

Baxter reached out to smooth the already smooth wall and smiled. "Yep. I still think something's missing. But this is One Awesome Thing, all right," he agreed.

"There was a second part to OAT," Waylon went on. "I used to make everyone say *And tomorrow's going to be even more awesome!* Every time. And tomorrow *is* going to be even more awesome. It's going to be the best day of my life."

"Right," Baxter agreed again. "Tomorrow we'll have him all day, from the minute we wake up. For good." He turned toward the alley. "Let's go make this happen."

13

When Waylon and Baxter tore up to the license office in City Hall, they found the clerk buttoning her coat.

Waylon slapped the twenty-dollar bill on her desk. "License. For our dog."

The clerk wound a scarf around her neck and pointed to a sign. HOURS: 9:00–5:00.

Waylon shook his head. He pointed to the clock, which read 4:58. He added a "Please?"

The clerk frowned at the clock and then unwound her scarf. She sat down. "Dog's name?" she grumbled. "Address?"

Waylon answered all her questions, and then she opened a drawer and took out a metal tag. She squinted at the numerals embossed on it, then copied them down onto a form. She handed over the tag. "Here's your license. If you lose it, it's another three dollars."

"We won't lose it." Waylon pulled the belt-collar from his pocket and worked the tag onto its buckle.

They ran the few steps to the station. At the door, Baxter side-mouthed a warning. "Act normal and let me do the talking. You know—the lying thing."

Waylon nodded and squeezed the dog tag. Their dog. In two minutes.

Baxter threw open the doors and they ran in.

The dispatcher opened the lock and the boys raced down the hall to the middle left-hand cage and skidded to a stop. The sleepy-looking bulldog inside lifted an eyebrow and then rolled over.

"Where's Eddy?" Waylon looked up and down the row of cages. He whistled, which set all the dogs barking. None of the barks was Eddy's.

"Where's our dog?" Baxter and Waylon demanded at once. They ran down to the Animal Control officer's office and banged the door open. *"Where's our dog???"*

Officer Sure-Not-Meg turned around. He pushed aside some papers and sat on his desk. He rocked around, getting comfortable. "The scrawny brown mutt?" he asked. "Oh, he's gone. I sent him off to the Springfield shelter today."

Waylon felt his heart slam against his ribs. Baxter's eyes bulged.

"What do you mean, gone?"

"He can't be gone!"

"Today's only Monday!"

"You said Tuesday!"

Waylon wasn't sure which things he had

yelled and which were Baxter's. It didn't matter.

"I did say Tuesday," Sure-Not-Meg agreed, leaning back. "But then I did a little research"—he tapped a stack of papers—"and it came to my attention that this dog has been escaping just before he's supposed to be shipped off. Sometimes on the *exact day*." He leaned in so close that Waylon and Baxter could see his scalp turning pink. "Now isn't that a coincidence."

Waylon gulped.

Baxter spun around. "Come on!" he cried.

They skidded down the halls. They found Officer Boylen pouring a cup of coffee in the break room.

"He took Dumpster Eddy!" Baxter cried as they burst in. "The new guy sent him to Springfield!"

"I heard. Sorry, boys."

Baxter threw his hands up. "You have to do something!"

"I'm sorry. Nothing I can do, son." Officer Boylen held out a box of muffins. "You guys hungry?"

Baxter waved the muffins away. "It isn't fair! He wasn't supposed to take him until tomorrow!"

Officer Boylen picked up a newspaper and shook it open. "Life isn't fair. You know that, son."

Waylon always hated it when grown-ups said *life isn't fair*. What it really meant was that grown-ups didn't care enough to fix something they'd messed up. If kids ran the world, it would be fair. Kids would *make* it fair. Baxter must have been thinking the same thing.

"You can do something, Dad. Go to the chief."

Officer Boylen put down his coffee and

folded his paper. He looked from one boy to the other, hard.

Waylon gulped. He knew Baxter's dad was a dad. But he was a policeman, too.

"The dog was taken to the shelter one day early, boys. One day. You want us to go get him just so he can leave again tomorrow? What's really going on here?"

Waylon and Baxter exchanged looks.

"It was my idea," Waylon started. "Don't blame Baxter."

"It's my idea, too," Baxter said. "We're both doing it."

"Doing what?"

Waylon drew a deep breath. "We're taking our dog. Forever. We've built him a home."

"You've *built* him a home? In Boston?"

Waylon straightened up. "An igloo."

"An igloo? You mean a snow fort?"

"An igloo," Waylon insisted. "Eddy can sleep in it. While it's winter. We'll make him something else later."

"We bought him a leash and a license and two weeks' worth of food," Baxter added. "We spent all the money we had. We're going to be with him every minute we're not in school. So you have to get him back! Before it's too late!"

"Okay, let's calm down, boys." Officer Boylen pointed to the table. "Take a seat."

Waylon sat when Baxter did, but the instant he did, his legs shot right back up. Sitting down felt like giving up on Eddy, and he wasn't doing that.

Baxter jumped back up, too. "I'll make the chief get him if you won't."

Officer Boylen grabbed the sides of his head and rocked it. Then he sighed and sat down. "Bringing him back wouldn't be fair to this dog."

He sighed again. "Boys, a dog needs a home. Safe. This Dumpster Eddy isn't going to be safe while you're at school every day."

Baxter folded his arms across his chest. "Lots of people have dogs and leave them to go to school or work. Those dogs are fine."

"*Inside*, son. They live inside. Or in pens, in good weather. You're talking about letting this dog run loose on the streets of Boston all day. I'm sorry, but there are rules against that for a reason. If you care about this dog, you've got to want him to have a safe home *inside*."

"But he *can* be inside," Waylon tried. "It's warm and dry in the igloo. We'll make a door for it and lock Eddy inside while we're in school if you want."

"Just come look at it," Baxter pleaded. "You'll see!"

Officer Boylen glanced at his watch. He

sighed once more and stood up. "I'll drive you guys home. If it will make you happy, we'll stop to see this igloo on the way."

When the cruiser turned into the dark alley, Waylon and Baxter gasped. They'd left the flashlight on, and the dogloo glowed a soft, snowy blue, with sharper light sparkling through the chinks between the blocks.

Baxter pulled his father down the path behind the Dumpster. "We made this," he said, spreading his arms over Eddy's home. "Every bit of it. Waylon and I."

In the glow from the dogloo's entrance, Baxter shone with pride.

Officer Boylen whistled softly. "Whoa. This is amazing," he admitted. "What a thing! I can see your police officer training has really paid off, Baxter. This certainly shows Perseverance.

And the Ability to Work as a Team." He put a hand on each of the boy's shoulders and beamed down at them. "Maybe you two *could* pull off this dog thing, after all. Mind if I look inside?"

As Waylon's dad crawled into the dogloo, Waylon and Baxter exchanged looks, their fingers crossed in bulky gloves. Officer Boylen was going to be impressed. He would see that they deserved their dog. And he'd go to Springfield and bring Dumpster Eddy back.

"See the water dish?" Baxter called into the tunnel. "A dog needs fresh water. We've got that covered."

"And the bed," Waylon added. "It's nice and warm."

There was no answer. In a minute, Officer Boylen backed out of the dogloo. In one hand was the yellow-striped pad. "What's this?" he asked.

"It's heated," Baxter explained. "See? We can

really take care of him. Tell him about the science, Waylon."

"A dog's temperature is one hundred and two degrees," Waylon said. "And snow is great insulation. This will be plenty to keep him warm. Plus we'll be hugging him. Hugging has been

shown to improve the immune system, too."
Waylon held his breath.

Officer Boylen raised the heating pad. "This
is great. Where did you get it, boys?"

"Baby Goods," Baxter said. "Also, we're going
to get some dog vitamins and—"

"Looks expensive," Officer Boylen cut off
his son with a curious expression. "I thought
you said you spent all your money on food and
a leash and a license."

Waylon gulped.

Baxter shot Waylon a look and then pointed
to the dogloo. "Um . . . did you see that flashlight in there, Dad? We're going to teach Eddy
how to turn it on. He's really smart—"

"How did you pay for it?" Officer Boylen's
face looked worried now. "How did you buy
something this expensive if you spent all your
money?"

Both boys looked over at Clementine's building, then down at their boots.

Officer Boylen crouched in front of them. "Just tell me. Did you boys buy this?"

"Um . . . yes?" Waylon said, while he felt his head shake *no*. His body froze, except for his hands, which floated to perfect Rogatory Position. "Actually . . . we . . . no."

Baxter stomped on his foot. Waylon's mouth snapped shut.

Officer Boylen stood up and turned to Baxter. "Get in the cruiser, son," he said.

14

Waylon got to school early on Tuesday morning after a night of no sleep, worrying about Eddy in Springfield and Baxter at home with his father. "What happened?" he asked, the minute Baxter showed up.

Baxter tossed his coat into his locker. He jutted his chin. "I didn't rat on Clementine."

"But what happened?"

"He kept asking how I got it," Baxter said, his face in his locker, "and I kept not telling.

After a while, my dad figured I stole it. I had to let him."

"So what did he do, Baxter?"

"He told me I had to return it. And I did—I put it at Clementine's back door this morning."

Waylon grabbed Baxter's shoulder and turned him around. "Did. He. Punish. You?"

At that, Baxter's face crumpled. He grabbed  his gut as if someone had kicked him. "He called the chief," he whispered. "He told him, 'My son isn't police material. Cancel the ceremony.'"

Baxter's shoulders shook as he walked into the classroom.

Waylon had never

seen a person look so heartbroken. Which he didn't understand. It wasn't as if anyone was actually going to let a ten-year-old be a real police officer. It was just a certificate that named him a junior—

Waylon stopped.

What if . . .What if Baxter felt the same way about becoming a junior officer for Chief Santos as he himself felt about becoming a junior correspondent for Neil deGrasse Tyson?

What if it had been Waylon's dad who had asked where they'd gotten the heating pad, and Waylon who had chosen not to rat on Clementine? And what if his dad had called up Neil deGrasse Tyson and said, *My son's not junior-correspondent material*?

Just imagining that, Waylon felt all the strength leave his body, as if there were drains in his heels.

Could that be how horrible Baxter was feeling right now? He didn't know. But he knew what he had to do.

When the dismissal bell rang, Waylon was the first out the door. He ran all the way to the police station.

Inside the lobby, he straightened up and drew a deep breath.

The station looked different this afternoon. The ceiling seemed extra high. The walls were lined with the portraits of past police chiefs who all seemed to be glaring down at him.

He walked to the dispatcher. "Is Chief Santos here?" Was it possible he'd just squeaked? He knew from *The Science of Being Human* that the vocal cords tightened when a person was nervous, and he certainly was nervous now.

"He's in his office. Go on in."

Waylon did.

Inside, he started talking before he could chicken out. "Baxter didn't steal it. We borrowed that heating pad from a friend, but the friend made us blood-swear not to tell, because the friend was afraid her mother would get all mad that their baby's heating pad had fleas or something. So Baxter didn't. Which showed good Police Officer Traits."

The chief leaned back and crossed his arms behind his head. "Good Police Officer Traits?"

"Baxter was Protecting a Source," Waylon explained. "And he Had a Partner's Back—mine—by Respecting my Different and Unique Ability not to lie. I can't, so Baxter knew that I'd tell about Clementine—I mean our friend—and then I wouldn't be Protecting a Source. So he was also showing Good Moral Judgment in Community Matters."

The chief cocked his head. "How do you know all this stuff?"

Waylon explained about helping Baxter study for the test. "Plus, police stuff is all he ever talks about. That kid is obsessed."

Chief Santos closed his eyes and nodded. Then he swiveled around in his chair. When he spun back, he picked up his pen and pointed it at Waylon. "I think you're right. I'll talk with

Baxter's father, see how he feels. Maybe we'll hold that ceremony tomorrow afternoon after all."

The chief made a mark on his desk calendar. Then he looked up. "And how about you? Seems you were part of this case. Is there anything the department can do for you in appreciation?"

Waylon knew that he should say something cheerful—like, *Wow, sure, Chief! Could I try on some handcuffs?*

But he couldn't do it. He only wanted one thing, and that one thing was gone forever. "No," he said and started for the door.

"Come on," the chief prodded. "There must be something the station can offer?"

Waylon turned around. "Dumpster Eddy." He hadn't meant to say it out loud, but what did it matter? "I just wanted our dog."

"I'm sorry, son," the chief said.

From the look on his face, Waylon knew he meant it. But it didn't help.

When he left the station, Waylon planned to go home. But his legs trudged right past his condo building as if they had a mind of their own.

Alien Hand Syndrome was one of his favorite Bizarre Conditions from *The Science of Being Human*, and Waylon was always on the lookout for another body part that could suddenly go rogue. But he knew it wasn't Alien Leg Syndrome he had. He knew where his legs were taking him, and he knew why.

When he reached the alley, he stopped beside the Dumpster.

He didn't know if he could bear seeing all the things in the igloo that would remind him of Eddy. But at the same time, the igloo was the only place he could be this afternoon.

He crawled in. "Hey!"

"Hey!" Baxter looked as shocked as Waylon felt.

"What are you doing here?"

Baxter tossed his arms up. "I have no idea. I tried to stay away, but I couldn't."

Waylon settled himself next to Eddy's bed. "Me neither."

Baxter got up and pushed off the top snow block. "What should we do with this place?" He poked his head through the opening and looked around. "We could knock off the roof and have a snowball fort. We could have some great fights."

"Epic," Waylon agreed with a sigh.

Baxter sat back down. "Or we could smash it."

Waylon shrugged. "Sure. Sledgehammers. All that snow flying."

They were silent for a minute. Then Waylon tugged his wallet free and slid out a picture: Waylon and Baxter, with Eddy between them. It seemed like years ago that Meg had taken it for them. He propped it up on the dog bed. "Or we can just hang out here," he said. "Remembering Eddy."

Baxter picked up the photo. "Best dog ever. I wish he were here."

Waylon sighed. "Me too. But . . . your dad was right. Eddy deserves a real home. Maybe he'll get adopted."

Baxter nodded. "He had some bald patches. He should have a place that's warm. With furniture to jump on. And floors, to keep his paws dry. And people around—Eddy loves people." Baxter's face grew worried. "But not criminals. Not someone who wants Eddy to be a lookout dog."

Waylon gazed up at the circle of sky. It was purple now, and a single star gleamed. "This has been the worst day of my life," he said.

But Baxter was already gone.

15

As Waylon hung up his stuff in the hall, he stopped. He sniffed. The air smelled like . . . air. "Dad?" he called.

His father came into the hall. He wasn't wearing the apron he'd had on for a week.

"You heard?" Waylon asked. "About your screenplay?"

Mr. Zakowski nodded. "It didn't sell. They thought that not enough happened in the plot."

Waylon patted his father's arm. "Are you okay?"

Mr. Zakowski looked surprised. "Of course. It just means another revision. I'll get started tonight. Your mom will be home around six. Pick out a couple of pizzas from the freezer."

After dinner, Waylon holed up in his room—he hadn't told his family about the plan to own Eddy, so now he had to be alone with his sadness about it not happening.

He did his homework, and then he got into bed with his book of famous scientists' biographies. Usually, reading them inspired him. But tonight, it seemed everyone he thumbed to had had a dog: Einstein had his Chico, Darwin had his Polly, and the Leakeys had five dalmatians. He put the book down.

The only not-terrible thing about this terrible

day was how happy his father was going to be when he found out that Waylon had helped him with his screenplay. Waylon lay back and imagined how it might go.

His father would drag himself into his studio and open his too-boring screenplay. A look of stunned gratitude would spread over his face when he got to the parts Waylon had improved. *This stuff's amazing!* he'd think. *How will I ever thank my son?*

Waylon hoped he was still awake when this happened. He could sure use a lift.

And then he heard it: his father's writing studio door opened and closed. He heard typing for a little while, and then . . . nothing.

Waylon sat up. He switched on his lamp.

He heard the studio door open again. Steps coming down the hall. A knock, and then his father stood in his bedroom doorway, the

screenplay in his hands, just as Waylon had imagined.

But something was wrong with the picture.

The look of stunned gratitude Waylon had imagined lighting up his father's face was missing.

Mr. Zakowski sat at the end of Waylon's bed,

frowning. He tapped his screenplay and raised his eyebrows. "Didn't we just have a conversation about this?"

Waylon knew what those raised eyebrows meant. "No, it's not the same thing at all," he said.

Mr. Zakowski's eyebrows elevatored up his forehead.

"Okay," Waylon admitted, "maybe a meteor crash is a *little* bit like Charlie's green slime. But—"

Mr. Zakowski's eyebrows shot to the top floor.

"Okay, okay. It's the same thing. But Dad, you need something to happen in your screenplay!"

"So everyone seems to think. But Waylon, you can't change someone's work. Charlie can't change yours, you can't change his, and you can't rewrite my script. I'll take other people's help, but the *co* in *collaboration* means *together*."

Waylon knew that. There were a lot of *co* words in science: *correlation, cohesion, coenzyme*. "I get it," he said. "Sorry."

"Look. I don't think the meteor is going to fit in, but the deep freeze afterward might be a good idea. Which reminds me: How did that dog like your igloo?"

Waylon flopped back, his arms over his head. "He never saw it. They sent him away too early."

"Too early? Too early for what?"

Waylon's stomach started to roll as he tried to think of an answer that wouldn't incriminate anyone.

But then he sat up. What did it matter anymore?

He told his father everything.

From the first time he and Baxter had busted Eddy out to yesterday's attempt, and all the times in between. All the not-exactly-illegal-but-probably-not-okay things he'd been hiding from his parents since September.

When he finished, he held his breath. Mr. Zakowski didn't look angry, but he was quiet for a really long time.

"I wish you'd told us," he said at last.

"I couldn't. It was Baxter's secret, too."

"Still. No more secrets from now on. Deal?"

"Deal."

Mr. Zakowski patted Waylon's foot and then stood up. "You know, maybe it wasn't so much that Baxter was a criminal that was bothering you. Maybe it was that what you were doing together made *you* feel like *you* were one. It's like in a screenplay: often, the very thing the main character doesn't like about someone is exactly what he's trying to avoid admitting about himself."

Usually Waylon stopped listening when his father got all writery. Writery stuff never made any sense. But this idea kind of did.

"Maybe," he agreed.

"Well, maybe now that you don't feel like you're doing something wrong, you and Baxter can be friends."

Waylon gave him a thumbs-up. Maybe they could.

Or maybe they already were.

16

Wednesday morning, Waylon went up to Charlie in the Pit. "We should try again," he said.

Charlie looked up warily.

"Look, there's no water on Pluto, and even if Char-Lon brought some, it wouldn't make slime, because it would evaporate immediately. But oil wouldn't. So what if we gave Char-Lon some oil, and he spilled that?"

Charlie brightened. "I could work with that.

Holy Kooka-Moly—can the oil be green?"

"Let's meet this weekend and research it. Together. The *co* in *Cosmo-Quest* means together."

Charlie went into 4B smacking his forehead. Waylon was about to follow, but Baxter came in

then. He was wearing a clip-on tie, and he smelled like aftershave.

"So your dad said okay?" Waylon asked. "You're getting the certificate?"

Baxter grinned. "The ceremony's today. I heard what you did. Thanks. The chief says he wants you there, too."

"Why?"

"I don't know. Four o'clock. Will you come?"

Waylon thought about it. Being in the station that would never hold Eddy again would hurt. But Baxter looked really hopeful. "Sure, I'll be there."

Six or seven police officers, including Baxter's father, were already in the chief's office, patting Baxter on the back, when Waylon walked in.

Chief Santos called everyone to order. Waylon edged to the back, where he couldn't see out the door. Because just beyond that glass door was the dispatcher's desk. And beyond that, the stray-animals lockup.

Where Eddy wasn't.

Even when Waylon heard someone come in and stand next to him, he kept his eyes locked on the front.

Chief Santos told everyone how hard Baxter had studied and that he'd gotten As on his written exams. He said that Baxter had run the obstacle course faster than anyone on the squad. Then Baxter recited the Officer's Code, and didn't get a single word wrong. Through it all, Sergeant Boylen stood beside his son, looking as if he could pop.

Waylon closed his eyes and imagined his

own mother with that look on her face on the day he was named junior correspondent on Neil deGrasse Tyson's show. His father would be proud, too, of course. But his mother, being a scientist, would really understand.

When Waylon opened his eyes again, the ceremony was ending. The chief pinned a badge on Baxter's shirt and handed him a framed certificate.

Then Baxter headed toward the back of the room. Waylon stuck out his fist for a bump, but Baxter walked past him. "Thanks for coming," he said to the person beside Waylon.

Waylon spun around.

There stood Mrs. Rice. Mrs. Principal-of-the-Whole-School Rice!

"Congratulations, young man," she said. "I knew you could do it. You are officially detention-free."

Waylon was so shocked, he just stared as she shook Baxter's hand and then left the station.

"Come on. Let's get out of here," said Baxter, tugging Waylon into the lobby.

"Hold on."

Baxter and Waylon turned back.

The chief had followed them. He nodded toward Waylon. "Didn't seem right to leave you out." Then he walked over to the lockup door and rapped three times.

The door opened.

There stood Sure-Not-Meg.

With a dog in his arms.

Who was Dumpster Eddy!

Eddy went berserk. He wriggled free and tore over to the boys, leaping from one to the other.

Waylon scooped him up. "You brought him back! You brought him back! How long . . . how long can he stay this time?" Waylon held his breath.

"Sorry," Officer Sure-Not-Meg said. "This dog can't stay in my lockup. He's not a stray anymore."

Waylon held Eddy tight to his chest, which felt like it had been kicked. "He's not?"

"No. This dog's been adopted."

Waylon felt his throat tighten and his eyes well up. He should just leave now. But his arms wouldn't unclasp around Eddy.

Besides, he had to know.

He locked his face and sucked in a breath. "Who took him?" he asked out loud. *Please let it be someone who deserves such a great dog,* he prayed silently. *Please let it be someone who will let Eddy run, who will sneak him scraps under the table, and who drives with the window open.*

Sure-Not-Meg tipped his head. Waylon followed his gaze to the dispatcher. The dispatcher crooked her finger at him. When Waylon got there, she pointed to the floor.

And there was Eddy's basket, lined with Waylon's own beagle pajamas. Hanging on a peg beside it was Eddy's retractable leash and a new red collar, with its shiny license tag.

"I figured it this way," the chief said. "I figured a police station that's just acquired a junior officer could use a junior canine officer as well. Problem is, we don't have the staff to take care of him. We'd be looking for someone to walk him every day, to feed him, brush him—you know what I mean. This dog can live here, but someone's got to own him. You know anyone up for this job?"

Waylon let Eddy scramble down to inspect his new home. "Me, sir. I volunteer."

He looked over at Baxter, still holding his certificate to his chest, but gazing down at Eddy, too. "With my partner, Baxter," Waylon said. "We volunteer to take care of this dog."

Baxter came over and crouched down with Waylon beside Eddy, who had curled up in his new bed. He fastened Eddy's collar around his neck. Baxter was smiling, but he looked worried, too. And Waylon knew why.

Dumpster Eddy was a runner. And the police lobby doors opened about a thousand times a day.

Just then, the doors did open. A woman stood in the doorway, struggling to get a stroller in.

Across from him, Baxter caught his breath.

Waylon's hand reached out to grab Eddy's
collar.

But he stopped himself. If Dumpster Eddy

was going to run when he had the opportunity—
if Waylon was never going to own this dog—he
wanted to know it now.

Baxter must have been feeling the same way.
"Go on, if you're going," he said to Eddy. "This
is your chance."

Eddy looked at the door. He sniffed the cold
air that came in and shivered. Then he looked
up at Waylon as if he was trying to tell him
something.

And Waylon didn't even have to go into
Vulcan mind-meld position to grok his message.
Are you crazy? Dumpster Eddy's dog-face said,
loud and clear to everyone in the room. *I've got
everything I've ever wanted right here.*

THE END

(almost)

There was just enough daylight left for a trip to the dogloo.

When they got there, Waylon unleashed Eddy. Eddy pranced over and circled the icy walls, sniffing every square inch he could reach. Then he zipped inside and popped back out, the rawhide chew clamped in his teeth.

"Genius," Baxter approved. "Your dog's a genius."

"He's your dog, too," Waylon said.

"Nah." Baxter held up his certificate. "This is going to take up a lot of time. I'll walk him with you, but he's your dog."

Dumpster Eddy! All his!

For a minute, Waylon didn't know what to say.

And then he did.

"Want to come home for dinner, Baxter?"

"Oh. Huh. Well, okay, I guess." Baxter didn't

sound very excited. But even in the darkening alley, Waylon could see that his new friend was smiling.

And that his new dog was lifting his hind leg. He was giving the dogloo the finishing touch it had always been missing: bright yellow against the blank white snow.

THE END

INTERESTING FACTS ABOUT DOGS (cont.)

10) Dogs can hear four times as far as humans.

11) Dogs curl up to sleep to keep themselves warm and protect their vital organs.

12) The moisture on dogs' noses helps them absorb scent chemicals.

13) Dogs prefer to poop in alignment with the Earth's magnetic field.

14) Dogs can see in black, white, blue, and yellow.

15) Dogs have at least eighteen muscles in each ear.

16) Dogs can feel jealousy.

17) The average dog can run about nineteen miles per hour.

18) Homo sapiens evolved with wolves, but Neanderthals did not. Neanderthals did not survive.